Kane

The First Blood Son

(Prequel to the Snow Blood series)

Carol McKibben

www.trollriverpub.com
Kane: The First Blood Son
Prequel to the Snow Blood series
Copyright © 2017 Carol McKibben
ISBN: 978-1-946454-28-7

Join the fun with Author Carol McKibben for giveaways,

updates and new release opportunities at:

http://eepurl.com/bAuq2b

Kane de Medici's thirst for knowledge leads him into the dark world of vampirism. Working as an apprentice to the great master, Leonardo da Vinci in 1503, he encounters Brogio, one of Florence's most wealthy bachelors. Their growing friendship coupled with strange events lead him to uncover Brogio's inconceivable secret. Brogio is a vampire, the very first vampire.

Kane's quest for endless learning has him propose that the vampire "turn" him so that he can become Brogio's first vampire blood son. Reluctantly Brogio agrees, but Kane's uncontrollable blood lust unleashes a plague upon the world.

This Snow Blood Series Prequel will delight fans of this beloved family of vampires.

1 – The Conversation

Kane awaited his future as he looked into Brogio's violet eyes. Eyes that shifted in color from red, then back to purple in an unnerving shimmer. Not at all human. Brogio's fangs extended, and his face contorted as if in pain. Surely opening his jaw that wide was excruciating. A momentary hesitation... Brogio paused and pulled back.

"You're not ready. Sit. Let's talk." Brogio pushed his six-foot-eight frame back a step. One hand swiped back long strands of silver blonde hair from his face. With a disappointed sigh, Brogio walked to the mahogany wood bar and pulled out two glasses and a bottle of wine.

Confused, Kane de Medici rubbed his dark eyes and stumbled to the plush, burgundy arm chair next to the roaring fire in the den of Brogio's Tuscany wine estate. Brogio shoved a glass of his finest Cabernet into Kane's hands and sat across from him. He eyed the dark haired young man's long six-foot-five body. Broad shoulders and a cleft chin were immediate outstanding features. Kane's dark eyes hinted at his extreme intelligence mingled with devilment.

"Tell me again why you would want to be an abomination like me. You are a descendant of the first bankers to the pope."

"Yes, the infamous de Medici. A notorious name I've tried to avoid all my life... criminals – all of them!" Kane sat down the glass of wine on a small mahogany table nearby and stared at the fire.

"But with you, the name could be synonymous with genius. You are apprentice to the great Leonardo da Vinci. Like da Vinci, you invent, paint and sculpt. You love architecture, science, math and engineering. You are devoted to literature, history and cartography. You have ongoing discussions with da Vinci about anatomy, geology, astronomy, botany and the two of you write together endlessly."

"Yet here I am, asking..."

"For Gods' sake, Kane, you're only 25 years old. Women faun all over you. They love your dandy ways, your elegant clothes, and your precise manners. Why would you want to become a blood sucker, like me?"

Kane's eyes sparkled above his wine glass. "Immortality. I want time. Time to learn. You know it's my passion. I want to watch things change and grow through the ages as you have. It's 1503. Can you imagine what the world will be like in the twenty-first century? The inventions? The science? The literature? The sheer knowledge that will exist?"

Brogio leaned forward. "It was that very genius of yours, and that of your Master da Vinci, that drew me to you. So I do understand. But once again, you must listen. When the blood lust consumes you, it must be controlled. If you run with it, the world will spread like a plague with my kind. If you purposely "turn" others, how long will it take for those progeny to get out of control?"

Kane leaned forward and twirled the wine glass in his fingers. "But, you grew up in an ancient time. You visited the Oracle of Delphin in 580 *before Christ!* You were here in 854 when Florence and Fieslewere united into one country. Look at how the world has changed since then! I want to see that. I want to be there. For history when it changes."

Brogio stood and faced the fire. He was silent for a moment then turned to Kane. "After I lost Selene, I slaughtered thousands of people in rage. I didn't allow any of them to live, except one. That's when I discovered that I could make others like me. She was beautiful, and I held her too closely, too long. Her companion cut my cheek with his sword when I attacked him. Upon her death, my blood dripped into her open mouth and revived her. I was fascinated by her transformation, but she became an uncontrollable ripper, her blood lust insatiable. I ended her to prevent my own discovery and more needless slaughter." The vampire ran his long fingers through his silver hair. "That's when I realized that the destruction of others wouldn't bring Selene back to me. If you hadn't discovered my nature, I wouldn't even consider making you my blood son. If I do turn you, you must allow me to control your blood lust. No one should have this curse without a choice."

"It was your own curiosity and quest for knowledge that gave you away." Kane rose and stood beside the vampire. "Why did you break into the Hall of Five Hundred that night?"

Brogio walked to the crystal bar to the left of the fireplace and poured more wine into the crystal goblets. "I had heard about *The Battle of Anghiari* da Vinci was painting and the running competition he had with Michelangelo. Each creating magnificence on opposite walls... I wanted to see for myself. I didn't realize anyone would be there."

"You could have said you were just curious. Why did you flee?"

"Would you have believed it? I was there in the middle of the night."

"No. But it wasn't because of the time. Da Vinci and I always work together at night there to avoid Michelangelo during the day. I had never seen anyone move that fast. When I ran outside, you were on the roof and then disappeared. I couldn't for the life of me figure out how you had gotten on that roof so quickly."

"Too bad you got a look at my face beforehand."

Kane placed his hand on Brogio's arm. "Will I be able to move that fast?"

Brogio smiled. "Probably. The ripper I created did."

"Will this actually work?"

"Turning you? I don't know. It's a risk we both take."

"Why did you seek an audience with da Vinci? Why didn't you stay out of sight?" Kane sipped his wine and looked around the opulent den with its rich burgundy and blue rugs, beautiful paintings and sculptures, and larger-than-life mahogany furniture.

Brogio smiled, and when he did, his violet eyes shined. "I wanted an audience with you and da Vinci. I thought to commission the master or his pupil to paint or sculpt me a piece of art. But I liked you instantly and returned and stayed for the friendship."

"You were lonely?"

"Mine has been an isolated existence."

"You have to hide?"

"I have been cursed by the gods. It took me centuries to learn to control my blood lust. I have created wine estates all over the world to be able to feed off the animals of the surrounding forest. But nothing, nothing quenches that thirst like human blood."

Both sat back down and sipped their wine. They remained silent as a servant dressed in black put more wood on the fire.

"Thank you, Ian." Brogio addressed the worker in a mild, familiar fashion.

Kane gave the servant a quick assessment. Ian stood tall, about an inch shorter than Kane. He had tied his long black hair with a rough ribbon that almost resembled burlap. The man's green eyes looked upon his master's guest with curiosity but quickly averted them when Kane returned his stare. Like most of Brogio's servants, Ian was quiet and didn't draw attention. However, the man displayed a strong, muscular upper body that ended in a V-shape because of his small waist. Strong enough to carry wine barrels, Kane thought. He certainly brought in a case full of wood for the fire with ease.

Ian left as discreetly as he'd come.

The blaze of fire as the wood caught cast strange shadows throughout the large room. A shiver ran through Kane's body. It was unclear to him if the shadows filled him with excitement or fear.

"You are a hypnotic being, Brogio. I was drawn to you immediately. You have the same love of knowledge, and you have gained so much of it. I wanted to be your friend." Kane leaned forward. "I want to be your blood son."

Brogio sighed.

"You have some type of magic in you." Kane smirked. "I thought you'd be perfect for Emily."

"Ah, yes. The twins... thought I was lacking in female companionship?"

"Perhaps."

"Well, you were wrong on that count. I have a broken heart, but it hasn't quelled my passion for the ladies. I tumble them then dine on them for dinner — never taking enough of their blood to kill them." Brogio rubbed his chin and smiled.

"Wait, you *do* drink human blood? How does that work?" Kane sat back waiting for his explanation.

"The trick is to only take enough and to stop. Then, I lick the wound, and it instantly heals. I compel them to forget."

"You... you make them forget? Could you not have compelled me to forget the suspicions I had about you?"

Brogio's smile was enigmatic. "Perhaps I wanted you to discover my nature. I don't know. It's difficult to hide one's existence... to not be yourself to at least... to someone."

"Explain to me again how you will make me like you."

"The only way I can turn someone is to *embrace* them. I can either give them my blood before I kill them or take them to the point of death and give them my blood. At least that is what I have deduced from my previous experience. I have chosen never to take someone against their will. That's why it is important that you are sure you want this. There is no reversal once it is done."

Kane stood up. "And your blood has healing power, right? Because when Victoria was thrown from her horse that day, I *knew* her neck was broken! You asked me to take Emily away so she wouldn't see Victoria in dispose. *But I saw you bite your wrist and put it to her mouth. You healed her!*"

"As luck would have it, the fall didn't kill her. She wasn't near death but would have been paralyzed. I healed her without turning her. And, ever since, you have pressed me about my abilities."

Kane walked with his hands behind his back, pacing in front of the fire. "So, somewhere inside of you, you wanted me to learn all there is to know about you. Help me to better understand how you were cursed."

Brogio hung his head. His voice was little than a whisper. "I fell in love with Selene, a maiden in Apollo's Temple at Delphi when I went for a reading with the Oracle. I stole her heart as well. The cursed god wanted her for himself. Ever since then, all of the gods have been my enemy."

"Selene? This is the woman you pine for?"

"Selene is more than just a trifle." Brogio's eyes flared red.

Kane raised his hands in supplication. "I meant no offense."

Brogio leaned back in his chair. "Artemis tricked us. She stole Selene from me."

"You fear I would suffer the same fate?"

"I would never let that conniving deity trick me again."

Kane remained silent. How many years had Brogio been alone? How many centuries? What had time done to his heart? His mind? "You long for a companion."

Brogio said nothing.

"All the more reason to make me like you." Kane stopped pacing. "If we are the same, you will be able to trust me to keep your secret."

Brogio stood. He took Kane by the shoulders and looked deeply into his eyes. "Are you sure this is what you want?"

"More than anything. Yes. Yes, I'm ready."

Without hesitation, the vampire's eyes blazed red as his fangs dropped. He embraced the handsome young man and latched onto his neck. Kane's brain went numb from the pain.

2 – The Aftermath

Kane woke in a darkened bedroom. Only a small candle illuminated the opulent space with its drawn brocade curtains, canopied bed, and lush surroundings.

Trying to sit up, Kane instantly folded over from the gut-wrenching agony that ran like fire through his veins. Everything hurt – his head, stomach, back, legs – he could not stop trembling. He cried out his pain as he tried to roll out of bed, only to collapse hard on the tapestry rug.

Brogio quickly entered the room, his feet a whisper on the mahogany floor. Setting down a tall glass, he rushed to pick up Kane — lifting him like one would a feather - and laying him back in the bed. Propping him up, he retrieved the glass filled with very dark red liquid. "Drink, my son. This will ease the pain."

Kane grasped the glass and gulped it down, draining the contents. Falling back, he felt a rush of euphoria and relief from his body spasms. "Why... the pain? Why so... much?"

Brogio placed a wet cloth on the suffering man's forehead and sat on the bed beside him. "It's the transformation. Each time I was cursed by another god with another burden, I experienced the horrible pain that you feel now. I am sorry. I thought it best not to burden you with this part."

"What was in the glass? It helped." Kane sat up, looking for more.

"It was my blood. I drained your body. You fed from my wrist just as you died. This glass of blood binds us together forever. This will put our minds in lock step. We shall have to see what gifts if any you possess as time passes."

Just then there was a knock at the door. "Master Brogio, are you all right?"

Kane sat up and listened. He could hear the man on the other side of the door. His breathing, his heart beat.

"I'm all right, Ian. There is nothing to worry." Brogio held Kane back and put a finger to his mouth.

Ian. Now Kane knew the servant's smell. Wood and wine. Ian... the servant who brought in fire wood last night. At the time he wondered at the servant's strength. Ian carried a barrel load into the room. He couldn't stop thinking about or hearing the blood rushing through Ian's veins. He could even hear the servant leave down the stairs. Incredible. Kane could sense all that, and through the door. He felt like a night walking predator with all the powers of a hunting bird. Sharpened eyesight. Keen sense of smell. Phenomenal hearing.

Kane ran his hands through his long dark hair, brushing it away from his face. He jerked in surprise as he heard the next words in his head. *The blood just offered will not be enough to sustain you. I will be providing you with my blood over the next several days until you are strong enough to hunt. You will need to feed further to complete the transformation and gain all of your strength.*

Kane looked closely at Brogio. The vampire's mouth didn't move. "I just heard you speaking to me in my head!"

Brogio threw back his head and let out a roaring laugh. *Excellent! I have always been able to read the minds of others. That's why I consulted the Oracle... to discover if I had psychic powers. Try answering me by thinking your words instead of saying them.*

Kane stared in shock at his vampire father. "I'll try." He closed his eyes. *Why do I feel this intense hunger?*

Brogio smiled. *It is the blood lust. You must learn to contain it as have I. My blood will quell your cravings in the next several moments. Later you can feed on animals or deplorable humans as long as you don't turn them.*

"I can hear you! This is amazing!" Stronger now, Kane leaped up on his knees onto the middle of the bed. His long shirt draped past his thighs, and he used the end of it to try and wipe his brow. "

Brogio stilled Kane's hand. *Understand that you are dead. There will be no sweat on your body, no illness, no breath. You can function as a man, thank the gods. But you must rest during the day and conduct all your activity at night. The sun will destroy you. Silver will poison you and eventually destroy you. You will need to feed nightly. You will make no other kindred. You will dine on animal prey. You will feed on the evil or the useless of society. You will kill any other only when you must to defend yourself. Those are the rules by which I exist. Understand?*

Kane stared at Brogio's strong, handsome face for a moment. *And the ladies that you bed and feed upon? Can I do that?*

Not until you can control your urges. It is too easy to let the blood lust consume you. Do you understand the rules and agree to abide by them?

Kane stood in the middle of the bed and swayed back and forth as he stared at his master. *Yes, father. I understand.*

3 – Kane's Lessons

So? How do I look?

I am not amused. Brogio stared at the mirror image of—himself. Kane's gifts came slowly but plentifully. One of them was being able to transform into anyone or anything. Demons, mythological beasts, people... anything Kane desired. Unfortunately, Kane desired to torment his father by playing Brogio's double.

But this could be useful.

You can imitate me, look like me, but you will never be me.

Of course, Father. Kane batted eyes disturbingly like Brogio's.

Brogio turned to go back into the studio where da Vinci practiced an experimental painting technique. But Kane, thankfully in his own form, stood before him.

And I see you've gained in speed.

Shall we go speak to da Vinci about that art piece you wanted to commission now?

"Gah!" A yelp alerted from the other room.

Brogio shot his hand out and grabbed Kane's shoulder, pinning his blood son to the spot. *Don't. Walk normally.*

Thank you, Father. Kane sucked in a breath. *Do you smell that?*

Control. Brogio could also smell the blood. *I will wait behind. You must control yourself.*

I'm all right.

You're shaking.

He's hurt. Kane wrenched out of Brogio's grip and went to the multi-talented master genius.

"Master?" Kane walked at a normal pace.

"Ah, my boy. I cut myself." Da Vinci held up his thumb. Blood gushed from it.

Kane rushed over with a piece of cloth to stop the bleeding. It took all his strength not to bite into da Vinci's hand.

"It's not so bad, Master." Not able to control it, Kane swooped down on the other man's finger and covered it with his mouth.

Da Vinci struggled and tried to pull away his hand. "What are you doing, my boy? Are you drinking the blood on my thumb?"

Kane managed to firmly lick at the wound and alternatingly swab the damaged appendage with the cloth. Between licks he muttered. "A new technique, Master. Hold still and let me stop the bleeding."

The thumb began to heal. The more Kane licked the more it healed. "There!" Kane looked into da Vinci's wide-eyed stare. "It's much better."

The older man held up his hand and wiggled his recently damaged appendage. His thumb was completely healed. No scar could be detected. "How? How did you do that?" da Vinci blinked in shock at his apprentice.

"I... it wasn't really that bad, master. I just stopped the bleeding." Kane dabbed his mouth with the cloth.

"What technique were you using?" da Vinci turned his hand over and again wiggled his thumb. "I could have sworn I almost cut my thumb off!"

"No, no. You were lucky. And, yes. Physicians are discovering that saliva has healing properties. I just took a chance that it might work." Kane turned away embarrassed at the obvious lie.

"Good work, young man. When we finish this mural, I'll have to look into it further."

Kane breathed a sigh of relief as his teacher turned to continue his painting.

∞

Kane, where are you? Did you forget the sun will destroy you?

Kane ran towards the estate. He was fast but not as fast as Brogio's blurring speed. He needed to be faster. *No. I just… I had to break off a conversation with da Vinci.*

The sun is rising!

I know! Kane's skin sizzled. The putrid smell of cooking, rotten meat trailed behind him. He couldn't ignore the itch or the burning. He was going to catch fire. The sun's first rays were moments away from blazing out from the mountains. He'd waited too long to return home.

He could no longer talk with the master painter through day break. Having to stop their conversations mid-way was a type of death. But Kane's transformation would be wasted if he couldn't get to Brogio's estate, and soon.

Hurry!

Kane pushed his legs, running down the path to the front door at a blinding pace. He rushed the door, just as a stream of light filtered over the hill and scorched Kane's arm.

"Ahhhowwwwww!" Kane screamed.

Quiet! Brogio commanded. *You'll alert the servants to your presence.*

Kane didn't much care who got alerted to what. His arm was in flames. Yet his master made a command, and he was unable to ignore it. Remaining silent he dashed into the coat closet and used a jacket to suppress his flaming arm. Kane shut the closet door as light started filtering into the main foyer.

You'll regret drawing attention to yourself if someone tries to find you.

Kane scoffed. *Only for half a second.* If that door opened he'd be charred brisket. *So now that I can no longer greet the sun, is this where I sleep?*

For tonight, stay where you are.

Kane's tempting sunlight became a torturous lesson. As he heard Ian walk back and forth down the hallway during the day, he prayed Brogio's helper wouldn't open the closet. The servant smelled of oak wood and red wine over the tantalizing aroma of blood. If not for the threat of death, he'd be tempted to open the door and sink his teeth into Ian's soft neck. But as the day passed, Kane's nerves were set alight, hoping Ian didn't open the closet door.

The hours crawled by as Kane sat uncomfortably in the closet. The burning sensation in his burned arm dissipated. Ripping away the material from his coat and shirt, he watched as his skin slowly knitted and healed. Soon he dozed and dreamed a strange dream. Brogio walked in front of him, motioning him to follow into the winery and down a dark stairway. They descended for some time, until the master vampire made a sharp left turn and pushed open a door. Two extra-long wine barrels positioned on their sides awaited them. Brogio walked to one of them and opened the top of the barrel which sported a hinge on one side. *This is where you will sleep henceforth.*

Inside the barrel had been converted into a luxurious bed. A lot more comfortable than a closet.

Kane's dream abruptly concluded with Brogio's voice running through his head.

You can come out now. Brogio's voice in Kane's head was becoming normal.

Are you sure?

Through the bond, Kane felt Brogio's huff. *Yes.*

Kane straightened his shirt and discarded the burned jacket. He opened the closet door just as Ian turned the corner and jerked to a stop.

"Master de Medici?" Ian eyed him. "Does Master Brogio know you're here?"

"Yes." Brogio trampled down the stairs, purposefully making noise. "There you are, Kane. Shall we?"

Without missing a beat, Kane grabbed another coat and closed the closet door. "Yes. A night out seems in order."

Ian stood there confused. Kane put his coat on as if everything were normal.

"Ian, I believe I hear your wife calling you." Brogio stared into the man's eyes.

Ian blinked several times. "Leslie?" He walked off like a man searching.

Did you just mind control him?

Ian? No. He and his wife have been with me for years. They don't question and remain loyal to me. Ian has a sharp mind and knows when not to press.

Tell me about Ian and his wife.

Brogio smiled. *Leslie is a beautiful, tiny woman with black hair and eyes. She is mulatto and always has a wide smile that makes dimples on her brown skin.*

Why have I never seen her in the house?

She works in the winery. Ian helps out there as well as in the house. I think they suspect that there is something 'different' about me.

Why?

Once when a barrel was about to fall on Leslie from an upper shelf, I sprinted to her side and caught it before it landed on her. A full barrel of wine weighs 600 pounds. Leslie asked how I could easily catch what takes two large men to carry. You should have seen the shock on her face.

How did you explain it?

Brogio shrugged. *I told her it was just years of managing wineries. Nothing amazing. I wanted to compel her, but Ian joined us, hugging her and thanking me. He said something like "Thank God you are safe, my wife." And she murmured she thought God had little to do with it and thanked me.*

Kane stroked his chin. *I imagine that they had quite a speculative conversation that evening.*

Yes, and it's been some time ago, so I trust their loyalty to me. Now, let's go quench our blood thrust.

As they walked out into the night, Brogio let Kane into his mind. He guided his pupil on how to stretch his senses out into the wild. Kane sensed game and started running forward. Brogio took hold of his arm.

It's best if you leave your clothes behind.

Eager to feed, Kane left his shirt, pants, boots and coat hidden under a bush. The feel of the air on his naked skin gave him the sense of freedom. He went after the animal with an eager joy. Kane was as untamed as a five-year-old with parchment and paint.

"You are as clumsy as a baby bear trying to swat flies." Brogio wrinkled his nose as he watched Kane take down a wild boar. "Don't just rip into the poor beast. Here, let me show you." Brogio pushed his son aside and ran a sharp fang along the pig's jugular. "Now, drink. It's a lot less messy. I'd think someone as meticulous as you about your appearance would have better table manners."

Kane rushed to the boar's throat and drank his fill. The euphoria overtook him, but this was not like Brogio's blood. The pleasure didn't last long.

It's not like before. Kane gave Brogio a disappointed look. *Is it because I'm fully turned?*

No. Brogio shook his head. He gave Kane a stern eye. *Animal blood is deficient in some ways. But this will teach you patience.*

Human blood is better. Kane remembered Brogio saying something about the difference.

It is... Brogio cut off Kane's next thought. *Soon. Be patient. I can't yet trust you to walk the streets of Florence for human prey. Remember, your actions have consequences.*

∞

After a month had passed, Kane was like an addict hungry for a drug. He begged to be allowed to find a poor vagrant to satisfy his need for human blood.

Brogio relented and accompanied Kane into Florence one evening. They strolled the cobblestone streets passing by ladies of the night on the arms of their patrons. Candle lamps dimly lit their way, and Kane watched with new wonder as nobles in horse drawn carriages carried on jovial conversations on their late night journey home from an evening with friends. He noted a few pickpockets hanging out on the street corners, all of them young and wary. A few brazen prostitutes approached them, drawn to the handsome picture they both presented and hopeful to spend a night with them, only to be rebuffed by a dangerous glance from Brogio.

Kane's body hummed in anticipation. His eyes flicked from person to person as they moved. A teenager, scrawny and quick with his hands, bumped into Kane.

"Sorry..." the kid mumbled and hunched in his coat, trying to look smaller than his already mousy appearance.

If not for his keen senses, Kane might have not felt the kid take his coin purse.

"Hey you!"

When Kane shouted, the boy ran. Pissed, he gave chase after the kid who melded into a crowd.

Kane, what are you doing?

That teenager took my money. Kane lifted his coat and breathed in the thief's scent where the boy crashed into him. With the tracking ability of a hound, Kane set off, following the trail. It led him to a pile of rubbish. He was in there. Kane started tossing garbage around when the kid jumped out and beat feet.

The chase was, once again, on. Kane took off after him, running into the street, down alleyways and through crowds.

For all your talents, you sure are having a difficult time keeping up. Brogio's chuckle reverberated in Kane's mind.

I'm trying not to give myself away.

Surely you can outsmart him.

"Maybe, if I weren't so hungry all the time." Kane said under his breath.

Which is why you need to be taught patience.

Kane groaned. He was unable to hide anything from his blood father. But privacy was important to Brogio, and Kane was often alone in his own thoughts. Tonight was an exception.

The boy's scent traveled up an apartment wall. How the hell did he climb that? *Is this kid human?*

Yes.

Impressive. Kane looked down the alleyway. The dark hall between buildings would keep his cover. Few pedestrians slipped past the outlet. Kane clawed his way up to the roof and watched as the kid leaped over to another roof. But this was where the boy made his mistake. He sought to slip away in the night sky, but without an audience, Kane could use his slowly maturing powers. And he did. Kane ran over the roof like a bolt of lightning crossing flat lands to the only available tree. He slammed the kid down on the tile roof.

"Return my coin purse, cretin." Kane shook the boy.

"I don't have it!"

"Liar!"

"Kane." Brogio placed a hand on his shoulder.

"This good-for-nothing stole my possession."

"Kane!" Brogio shoved his blood son on his back. *Remember what I told you. About being careful.*

The teenager skidded back like a spider. "What the hell are you?"

Brogio turned to boy. "What's your name?"

The little ruffian swallowed, his eyes going wide. "Joseph."

"Well, Joseph, I suggest you don't provoke things like us."

Kane stood up. "If you're going to kill him, I want to do it."

"No." Brogio swept his arm out. "You have to be sure no one will miss him. Though, he looks like an orphan."

"Then that means no one will miss him."

"That's not true," Joseph said. "I have... I have people that will come looking for me."

Brogio bent down and stared into Joseph's eyes. "That's not exactly the truth, is it." The master vampire held out his hand. "Hand it over, boy."

Joseph reached inside his coat and pulled out a coin purse. Just before the bag reached Brogio's hand, Joseph tossed Kane's coin purse. In a blink, the boy was charging down the wall.

Kane jumped up.

Leave him.

But he knows about us.

What he knows is that none would believe his story.

You don't want to erase his memory?

Why? Brogio chuckled. "Do you want to chase after him again?"

Kane scoffed. *I was only trying to stay discreet.*

As you should.

Then why let him go?

He's harmless and not our concern. Brogio stepped over to the edge and dropped down to the alley floor.

Kane followed suit. Brogio sniffed the air. *Smell that?*

Kane sniffed, and his fangs immediately sank below his lower lip. *Human stench.*

Yes, midway, leaning against the wall. Take him, but do not let him live.

Kane rushed to the snoozing beggar's side. The stench of the man made him almost gag, but he ignored it, covered the man's mouth with a large hand, and grabbed his prey. Sinking his fangs into the peasant, he drained him. Afterward, he broke the man's neck to make sure he wouldn't survive. Overtaken by the ecstasy of human blood, Kane fell to his knees, slid down the wall and lolled in a euphoric state.

Brogio joined him, picked the body up and carried it through the back alley, dumping it into the Arno River. Returning, he picked up his progeny and pushed him against the wall. *I just disposed of the body. This is the way it has to be done. Do you understand?*

"Y... yes." Kane mumbled aloud.

I would prefer you stick to the animals of the forest, but when you must, only do so in the dead of night and to those no one will miss.

Like that boy, Joseph.

Brogio smirked. *The price for his thievery should not be death.*

Kane laughed. *Don't worry, Father, I won't hold a grudge.*

4 - Kane's Mistake

Kane rose from the bed, slipping his clothes back on. His conquest of this night snuggled under the rich down comforter and large, soft pillows. Her slim legs dug deeper under the sheets. He leaned over the bed, checking for bite marks on her neck. Her skin was flawless. Not even a mark.

He quietly exited the room knowing when she woke she would only remember that she had a good time. Nothing more. Not even his name.

Kane hurried downstairs to ready himself for his work with da Vinci. Brogio blocked the landing by standing on the last step.

Facing his blood son, Brogio's expression filled with concern. *You stray too far afield in your search for blood, Kane. If you are caught, you will expose our kind.*

I am being careful.

Brogio shook his head. *In your blood lust, you have become reckless. Your purpose of gaining time for knowledge has taken a back seat to your thirst for blood. What about your work with da Vinci?*

Kane turned on his maker. *I will not be caught.* His dark eyes sparkled with rebellion. *I see no reason why I can't enjoy feeding. You know that I am working with da Vinci at night enough hours to satisfy him.*

Brogio stepped off the stairs and let Kane pass.

Stomping off, Kane left for the night. But a part of him feared Brogio might be right. He could not get enough blood. Not just blood. Human blood. His thoughts carried him to the steps of Master da

Vinci's workshop, where he did not find the painter, but an older friend.

Mia was the widowed wife of a minor nobleman and barely had anything left of her late husband's estate. She relied on what her family could give and any other favors she gained from friends. Kane had always given her what he could. She'd been good to him when her husband was alive, and he sought many times to help her now that the tables had turned.

"Mia, what brings you to da Vinci's workshop?" He held out his arms, eager to scent the air with her enticing human odor.

She clasped her hands together as she stood up from the stone bench where she had been waiting. "You actually."

"Me?" He engulfed her with his arms. "What trouble are you in?"

She looked miserable but returned his embrace. "Funny you should ask."

Kane pulled her back. "Mia, what's wrong?"

The lonely window shook her head and sniffled. "My family, they can't give me my stipend this month. Clara has a new baby, Dan is out of work. They have nothing for me. I came to beg myself for favors. I am sorry, Kane. I don't know who to go to."

Compassion clashed with hunger, and Kane fought to regain his control. Her desperation was a siren song to the deep pit of his stomach begging to bite into her. "Mia, don't be so stricken. I can help you."

"No!" Mia grabbed his arms. "No, Kane, you have helped me enough. I will not take advantage of your kind nature."

"Nonsense." He smiled as his quick mind worked to solve both his and her problems. This could be an answer to his hunger situation. "I may have a solution. Something that benefits both of us."

Mia pulled back. Her eyes appraised him with weary resignation. She retained some dignity, but she was desperate. "Go on."

Ahhh... how would he explain? "I find myself in a peculiar predicament." He paused watching her.

She again clasped her hands tightly together and waited.

"I would like to propose a trade."

Her lips curled. "A trade?"

"Yes."

"Skin privileges?"

"Of sorts." He laughed. Oh, dear sweet Mia. How would this dark-haired beauty react to his new-found habit?

Mia reached out and touched his hand. "Whatever it is, you can trust me. I won't say a word. Even if I refuse."

Beautiful and smart. Kane breathed in, though not needing air, he found it harder to break free of human unconscious functions, like breathing and blinking.

"I worry you may think harsh of me."

"Everyone has secrets, Kane." Mia bent her head in demur shame. "Some secrets are whispered from the mouths of those you don't even know."

He caught her meaning. Society had been cruel to Mia. A misplaced word became rumor that turned into gossip and then fact. Mia was not the harlot everyone saw her as. She was a proud woman. But everyone assumed she'd given her body to men to pay for her living. It wasn't true. But because of rumor Mia's chances of remarrying were not high.

"Blood," Kane blurted out.

Mia looked up and blinked. "Blood?"

"Yes, I need blood."

She appraised him, and then said, "My blood?"

Kane nodded.

"How much of my blood?"

"A vial or two would do." Kane rushed to answer trying not to spook her. "Once or twice a week perhaps?" Would it be enough to satisfy him? It would have to.

"Is this for your work with da Vinci?"

"Ummm…" Kane hated lying to her, so he smiled for forgiveness instead.

"No matter." She waved.

"I will replace your stipend. Make sure you're taken care of. I won't take too much." How would he retrieve his payment? Would biting her and licking the wound be enough? He feared manipulating her mind too much would make her stupid. Perhaps even cause irreprehensible damage to her brain. He could not risk doing that to her. As long as she thought he was conducting experiments, he could hide the true nature of his request.

"I agree. Shall we start?"

∞

Mia's blood sang through his veins. And still it was not enough. He'd taken very little, but the sweet nectar enticed him more. Oh, the ecstasy was divine. He could easily drink the red water of life for days. He'd left Mia dazed and somewhat confused. He compelled her to forget sinking his fangs into her lovely white neck. Instead, he suggested he made a small incision in her neck and drained it into a small vial. He left the tiniest nick to ensure she believed him and handed her a handkerchief with which to dab it.

Afterward, since he hadn't been able to find da Vinci at the Hall of 500, he walked the streets of

Florence. A young woman soon came alongside him.

Beautiful, she moved around him like a cat, rubbing against him playfully. "What's your pleasure, handsome? You're too gorgeous to be alone tonight, don't you think? Got a girlfriend?"

"No." Kane watch the blood pulse through the artery in her neck and could feel his control slipping. He focused on conversation to alleviate the blood lust. "You're younger than most of the ladies of the night I've seen around here."

"Awh. I've been around. I'm 21 and know how to please you." She rubbed a long fingernail under his chin and came closer so he could get a better look at her partially bared breasts.

Kane grabbed her by the throat, surprising her.

She squealed as he ran his tongue down the side of her chin and rested his mouth just at the pulsating artery of her neck. He mumbled against it. "What will it take for you to join me at my... old... apartment? It's just near the Hall of 500."

She stood on her tip toes and wrapped her arms around his neck, running her hands through his long hair. "Why 75 Lira will buy you the night."

He smiled down at her. His anger at displeasing Brogio bubbled into heated blood lust. He picked her up and ran with her to the rooms that he still kept near his work. Setting her down to remove the key from his pocket, he unlocked the door, picked her up again, kicking the door behind him. He chuckled as he thought about the night he had compelled his landlord to invite him into his own apartment once he realized that the actual owner had to issue an invitation to enter.

He sat the wench down so quickly that she staggered and fell onto a nearby threadbare sofa. She again squealed her delight and began to remove her boots, legs straight in the air.

Kane moved to his meager bar and poured them each a glass of wine. As he handed her a glass, he reached down and ripped off the stocking that she struggled to remove.

She laughed and chugged down the wine. Pulling on her other stocking, she flung it to the other side of the room.

He gulped his wine and set the glass down on a nearby end table.

With one quick movement she pulled out a small knife and cut the laces of her bodice and exposed her chest to him. "You like?"

Kane growled as he buried his face in her breasts. Scooping her up, he carried her to a small bed in the next room and threw her down. Her laughter filled the room as he reached down and ripped off the rest of her dress, exposing her naked body.

His blood lust came to a boiling point. He fell on her and took her in a fit of passion. As he pounded into her, he couldn't stop himself. He latched onto her throat with his fangs.

She cried out and struggled. "Oohh! What are you doing? That hurts. Stop!"

The more she resisted him, the more frenzied he became, draining her body of its blood. Soon, Calliope stopped moving.

Kane instantly realized his mistake. He slashed his own wrist with his fangs, forgetting Brogio's warning and thinking he could save her by dripping his blood into her open mouth. After several minutes passed, Calliope stirred and sighed.

Satisfied and in a euphoric daze from her blood, he fell back and slept.

He awoke in the early morning hours and reached for her, but she had disappeared. With no time before the sun rose, he ignored his instinct to look for her and returned to Brogio's estate just as the flaming orb began to streak across the sky.

The next night as they emerged from their sleeping chambers in the winery next to the estate house, Kane contritely apologized to Brogio but couldn't resist the urge to taunt his maker. *I have done no wrong. I will return to the forest at night with you to stay in your good graces, Sire.*

Brogio raised an eyebrow and looked deeply into Kane's dark eyes. *We will see if your nightly forays into Florence have created a problem.* The master took hold of his blood son's shoulders. *But I sense you have unleashed a scourge upon this world, Kane.*

∞

Kane found Calliope on the arm of a young suitor a fortnight later on the streets of Florence.

"Calliope, may I speak with you alone for a moment?" Kane blocked the couple's passage.

"Why, Kane, my *noble friend.* Anything you say to me can be said in front of my mate Anthony." She glanced sideways at the slender young redheaded man next to her.

"No. It is a matter of some importance. I want to inquire as to your health."

Calliope threw back her head and laughed, and her young partner joined her.

In an instant, Kane pushed her companion aside and grabbed the girl's arm, pushing her into the alley.

She turned on him, flashing fangs, her eyes glowing red. "Thanks to you, I've never felt better!"

A shiver went up Kane's spine as he realized what had happened. Pushing Calliope closer to the wall, he asked through gritted teeth, "Have you been feeding off your clients?"

"Not just feeding off... I found I could make them like me! Now back off! I have an entire brood of feeders to look after. In fact, I think I'll grow me an army! We're discovering new power over humans every day! You should join us. We can eat our way through all of Italy!" Her laughter followed Kane as he backed away from her. Turning, the redhead flashed his fangs at Kane.

Kane turned and sprinted with lightning speed to Brogio.

Falling through the front door of the estate, he stumbled toward his maker who stood in front of the fire. No words were necessary. Brogio already knew what Kane had inadvertently unleashed.

The look on Brogio's face turned Kane to stone. He halted in the middle of the room, shoulders slumped, hands beseeching his master and reverting to spoken words. "I... I made a mistake. I..."

Brogio responded with his own words. "You said you understood, but obviously you don't. I wanted to trust you. You have betrayed me, Kane. Leave now. I do not know when I will be able to look upon your face again."

"But, father... I meant no harm. It was an accident."

Brogio's thoughts tore into Kane's head. *LEAVE NOW! DO NOT RETURN UNLESS YOU ARE SUMMONED!*

Black blood tears rolled down the chiseled white skin of Kane's face. He knew it was useless to argue. Turning on his heels, he quietly slipped out the door into the night.

∞

Kane's black leather riding boots crunched on the gravel of the driveway leading away from Brogio's estate. He realized that as his first task he needed to locate a secure resting place before sunrise. With his vampire speed intact, he raced to the Hall of 500. The building had a ground-level vault housing a number of coffins for the structure's builders, Simone del Pollaiuolo and Francesco Domenico. Their bodies would someday rest there, but for now he would make use of one of them.

"Good evening, sir."

Da Vinci greeted Kane with a wave of the hand as he entered. He had been experimenting with an encaustic technique that wasn't working well on the wall designated for his mural. Kane busied himself for a while until da Vinci was absorbed in his experiment. He then slid into the unsecured vault. He found two elegant coffins covered with cloth. Removing it from one of them, he discovered the perfect place for his daytime rest. The elegant walnut coffin was carved decoratively and had piles of padded black satin in which he could rest with the lid closed. Noting its convenience, he closed the lid and slipped out of the vault to continue his nightly work. In the coming days, he would determine how to get back into Brogio's good graces.

The next evening at sunset, Kane arose from the surprisingly comfortable coffin in the pitch black vault. He used caution to crack the door in the possibility that da Vinci had worked throughout the day. The multi-faceted genius had apparently left in a rage, leaving the floor next to his mural splattered with paint and various substances. A can of brushes had been thrown against the floor and lay in disarray. Kane stretched and stooped to pick them up. He paused for a moment and considered whether to feed on some poor beggar or go to the woods surrounding Brogio's estate to prey on the night animals. *If I am going to make amends to him, I'd better do what he would prefer.* With that thought, he glided across the floor and out into the night.

His lightning speed brought him to the forest. Carefully removing and folding his clothing next to a large Italian Cypress tree, he pushed them into intersecting branches. Sniffing the air, he caught the scent of a wild boar and followed the smell to his prey. With almost invisible speed, he took down the creature, slit its jugular, and drained it of every last drop of blood. Wiping his mouth with the back of his hand and casting the beast aside, he turned and looked into the purple eyes of his blood father.

Kane paused but couldn't help himself. He taunted, "Checking up on me, father?"

Brogio's eyes glowed red. "Speak to me telepathically."

Taking a step back, Kane bowed his head. *Brogio, please... I apologize for my mistake. How can I gain your good graces again?*

You have no idea what you've done, Brogio glared at his blood son. *My senses tell me that you have created an army of uncontrollable rippers who will kill humans without reservation.*

But...

Silence. Go about your existence for now. I need time to assess the situation. I will call you if and when I know more. As much as I hate to admit it, I might need your help. Brogio backed away into the night.

Kane closed the distance to the nearest lake, jumped in, and washed off the blood and dust of previous days. Heading back to collect his clothes, he sprinted to the Hall of 500 to work with da Vinci.

As soon as Kane entered the foyer, da Vinci called out. "My dear boy, is that you?"

Kane washed his face with a hand. "Yes, Master."

"Ah, good. Good. Will you fetch me a ladder?"

Kane turned the corner to the Great Hall... and found da Vinci held by a contraption that seemed attached to the vaulted ceiling.

"Master!" Kane rushed to the ladder up against the book case and pulled it from its track. "What are you doing up there?"

"Ah... I got tired of painting." Da Vinci swung from a harness. He seemed safe enough.

"You've found yourself in dire straits, I see." Kane held the ladder steady against the wall even though he could hold it well enough in mid-air.

"The ladder fell away just at the wrong moment." Da Vinci placed his feet on the ladder and unhooked the harness. "Dire straits or not, this contraption will change mankind."

"Or kill you," Kane mumbled.

When da Vinci climbed down to safety, he grabbed a book and scrambled around in aimless wanderings.

"Looking for a quill?" Kane searched with da Vinci.

"You know me well."

Searching, Kane picked up a book titled *Wrath of the Gods*. "What is this doing here?" He held up the book.

Da Vinci absently scanned the tome. "Ah, interesting book you have there."

Curious, Kane opened the book and scanned for Artemis. The goddess that punished Brogio to his fate. Then he learned of Apollo, her twin brother. As he searched the pages at the mention of their father, Zeus, Kane reached for a chair and sat.

"What do you make of it?" Da Vinci peered down at Kane.

"Fascinating. Do you really think Hades guards the souls of the dead?"

"Perhaps one day we shall find out." Da Vinci's eyes looked blood shot. His face drooped in exhaustion.

Kane looked at the time. He'd been sitting in the chair for five hours. "Why didn't you tell me the time?"

"You were studying."

"This is not science." Kane set the book down.

"Ah... is it not?"

He had to go. He needed to feed and hide from daylight. "Perhaps we can speak of it another night. I apologize. I've not been much of an assistant tonight."

"Nonsense." Da Vinci waved him away. "Knowledge comes from many places."

Before Kane could exit, da Vinci held up one finger, deep in thought. "Before you go, my boy, take a look at this material. It's a combination of complex copper carbonate, powdered glass that

I've colored with blue cobalt, azurite, and charcoal."

Kane took the bucket that the master handed to him and sat back down on his stool. "Has the Greek pitch I applied to the plaster adhered well enough to your liking for this?"

"Yes. It has been drying for days. It should be a good base for this paint I've concocted."

"You've brought back an ancient encaustic method of coloring stucco."

"Yes. The problem is that in experimenting with it, the paint drips because it's so damp. I tried to heat it with a brazier, and that made it worse."

Before Kane could respond, Brogio's voice rang inside his head. Come to me now, Kane. It is time you made amends for the problem you have created.

Kane jerked up off his stool and spilled the paint materials on the floor.

"Be careful, my boy," da Vinci cautioned. "God knows if that stuff might explode."

Kane cleaned the mess he'd created and then approached his instructor. "Sir, I have an important errand to run. Do I have your permission to leave for the night?"

Da Vinci turned to him and patted his student on the shoulder. "Go ahead, boy. You've been putting in long hours. I can't for the life of me figure out why this damn material won't adhere to the wall properly." Da Vinci turned away and was once again lost in his experiment.

Kane rushed out the hall's front entrance. One hundred feet down the street, he saw a distorted man take hold of another and drag him into the alley. The victim's screams echoed throughout the street. Kane was on the attacking creature in seconds, tearing him off the screaming older man.

Without a thought, Kane ripped the other vampire's head off his shoulders.

The creature's terrified victim crouched against the stone wall. Fortunately, the other vampire hadn't had time to finish his attack. The man was unscathed. Kane leaned into him, his hands on the wall above the man's head. Peering intently into the human's eyes, he commanded, "Forget what you have seen here tonight. Go to your home believing that you had an uneventful walk."

The man slowly shook his head in the affirmative. As Kane turned around he met the eyes of a soldier. A familiar face. His cousin Marco stepped forward and eyed Kane for some moments before he nodded. "Cousin Kane."

"Marco?" Kane pulled back. "What are you doing here?"

Just then a band of soldiers brawled with one of Calliope's Rippers. Marco spun around, lifted his spear high and stabbed the creature through its neck with one blow. "I told you to take off their heads."

The soldiers saluted Marco and started off toward screams in the distance. The streets were a mess. Kane could smell the blood splattered on the streets. Italy was becoming a slaughter house. Marco assessed Kane through dispassionate, calculating eyes. How much had his cousin seen? Would he have to erase his memory?

"The Medici have returned to Florence," Marco finally said.

"I see." Kane measured Marco with the same manner as the soldier had leveled his gaze with accusatory disapproval. "I'd heard a Medici is now Pope Leo X."

Marco breathed in relief. Whatever test he'd had in his mind, Kane passed. "Be careful, cousin, the Spanish and the papal armies are here to fight whatever monsters these are."

Kane hung his head. He and he alone was responsible for the destruction, the monsters gone rampant, the loss of life. "Don't let them bite you."

"We know." Marco's accusing glare returned. As if to say, what have you done, Kane?

"Be safe, cousin."

Marco held out his hand, and they clasped forearms. "Seems you can handle yourself, but may the grace of god be with you."

"I doubt he'd grant me any favors."

Marco grunted, and then he was gone.

∞

Brogio opened the door just as Kane was about to knock. It was uncanny how Brogio sensed his every thought and movement. Brogio's purple eyes bore into him, causing momentary pain.

"You've unleashed quite a disaster, Kane." The master vampire widened the door and nodded toward the den.

Kane stepped through the doorway and headed to the ever-present fire. Avoiding the conversation at hand, he looked to the flames. Why have such a thing since their kind can feel neither feel warmth nor cold?

I like to watch the flames.

Brogio knew his every thought. That fact chilled Kane down to his cold bones. He knew that he had to forever be forthright with his maker or suffer the consequences.

I know it's bad. I just pulled a rabid ripper off a victim outside of the Hall of 500.

Brogio stepped to the bar and poured them both a cabernet into crystal goblets. Handing one to Kane, he sipped his own. *Calliope's coven has grown to over 5,000. They are like a disease spreading throughout the city. Soon, they will go beyond.*

Kane's hand shook as he tried to remain calm and lift the wine goblet to his lips. *What can I do? How can I help?*

Brogio brushed a long stray hair behind his left ear. *Fight fire with fire. A cliché but one that is effective.*

What do you mean? Kane turned, took a large gulp of his wine, and stared into Brogio's eyes.

We will create covens of our own to overmatch their strength. They have to be terminated.

Kane sloshed his wine in surprise. *Create more vampires? But... I thought...*

Brogio held up his hand impatiently. *Thoughtfully create those who will follow my rules. No ripping, but only after we have them under control. No turning others after that.*

It would take years. Calliope is indiscriminate.

Brogio smiled. *Ah, yes... but illiterate and stupid. She will be fighting centuries of learned strategy and wisdom.*

But numbers can overpower.

Brogio sipped his wine and turned to the flames. *We will tap those we know who want what we have to offer. We will contract with them to uphold my rules. We can multiply like rabbits in a heartbeat if I so wish it. Calliope doesn't have my vast connection of people, and she is creating mindless drones. We will invent an army.*

Okay. I trust you, Father.

Who do you know that you might bring here?

Marco comes to mind. Perhaps Mia. I can find others.

Brogio turned away from the fire and sat across from Kane. *Tell me about Marco and Mia.*

A cousin of mine. A soldier, but he's like me. A Medici but another black sheep of the family. He desires more than he has.

And you trust Mia?

Yes. I know she's unhappy with her situation. I can convince her.

All right, I have three others in mind — Alexander, Ian, and Leslie. So we can begin with those five.

Who is Alexander?

Brogio sipped his wine thoughtfully. *I met him several years ago. He is an officer in the Pope's army. I actually bumped into him at a social event. We both had interest in the same lady at the party, even though his intent was most likely more honorable than mine. He kept competing with me for her as a dance partner. He was clearly besotted by her.*

Kane pressed. *You mean a human man actually attracted her more than you did?*

Brogio smirked. *No actually she preferred me, but I felt sorry for Alexander. We ended up drinking together. Of course, he got drunk and revealed that he had been passed by for a promotion and was devastated because the army was his life.*

He became your friend? Kane gulped down the rest of his wine.

Yes, I have him over for dinner occasionally, and we sometimes meet out for drinks. I think his ambition to lead would come into play well for us.

As Kane thought another name came to mind.

Brogio plucked it from his thoughts. *Joseph? The boy thief?*

Shall we begin?

5 – The Extension of Brogio's Kindred

Brogio and Kane went about it with reluctance. Difficult at first, it became easier as they amassed an army of kindred. The first was Alexander.

Brogio invited the handsome redheaded, blue eyed soldier to dinner at his estate house. Upon hearing the vampire's incredible story and asking all the inquisitive questions that Kane had previously, Alexander replied, "The promise of eternal life leaves me breathless and excited. But, the chance to lead a legion of vampires with extraordinary power appeals even more. I am ready now!"

Ian and Leslie soon followed.

When he called them to his house and revealed his true nature, they appeared unsurprised but nervous. After a full explanation of vampire characteristics, they looked at each other knowingly.

Ian turned to the creature he had served for a decade and smiled. "We knew you were not of this world, but what you are is beyond our simple comprehension."

Brogio's violet eyes glowed red, and Leslie nervously took her husband's hand. He placed his gaze upon the woman and asked. "What questions do you have of me, Leslie?"

She didn't hesitate. "Has your long life been a happy one?"

Brogio's eyes returned to normal. He shook his head. "When I had the love of my life with me, it was like no other. Without her, it has been one of loneliness."

Ian interjected. "But has your life of wealth not given you some comfort?"

Brogio sighed and looked at them both in the face. "If I had my Selene with me, then the wealth that I enjoy would buy us the freedom of choice to do whatever we wanted. The two of you have each other, and you could have that freedom as well."

"What consequences could we suffer as vampires?" Leslie leaned toward Brogio.

"I won't lie to you. You can suffer the true death. A wooden or silver weapon through your heart, the severing of your head, sunlight... these are all things that can destroy us. Now you understand why you never see me during the day. We must rest in the dark away from sunlight at that time. But your superior speed and strength, access to my knowledge, and the protection of those within our coven will prevent those outcomes."

Ian searched his wife's face for her answer. She gave it with a slight nod of her head.

Ian reached out to shake Brogio's hand. "A life of adventure and an ability to better ourselves would be ideal for us."

Next, Kane went in search of Joseph, the scrawny pickpocket who spent his days on the streets of Florence. It was easy enough for Kane to find him working the streets. One night while he was busy fleecing innocent bystanders, Kane grabbed him by the scruff of his neck. "Want to really live a life of mystery and intrigue, boy?"

"Hey, get your hands off me!" Joseph struggled against the other's superior strength. The boy's eyes widened when he recognized the man whose dark brown eyes glowed red.

"Come with me, young man. Willingly."

Compelled, Joseph nodded his agreement and walked calmly with Kane to the carriage that awaited them.

Upon meeting Brogio, who once again terrified the boy, his mischievous spirit and lowly prospects in life made vampirism appealing to him.

"You'll no longer need to steal for a living. Your needs will be taken care of," Brogio filled the boy in as he sat eating a plateful of sweets that Ian had served him.

Joseph looked around, gobbled down the crumbs from his dish, and said "more please."

By the end of the night, he joined the growing coven with pleasure.

Kane approached Mia, who had continued to hold up her bargain for blood with Kane but rarely remembered how he had extracted her blood. When Kane knocked on the door of her shabby but immaculately clean apartment, she registered shock. "Is it time for payment so soon? I just saw you a few nights ago."

"No. I would like to invite you for a late dinner at my friend Brogio's estate."

"Brogio?" Mia's face flushed. "He is one of Tuscany's most enigmatic but eligible and wealthy bachelors. He is your friend?"

"Yes. Would you like to see his estate?"

"Would I. I have heard it is glorious. Does he have a last name?" Mia twirled in excitement.

Kane laughed. "He only goes by Brogio. I think it's short for Ambrogio."

"When is the dinner?"

"Now."

"Now? But I have nothing appropriate to wear." Mia ran to her meager closet searching for anything suitable.

Kane stepped through her doorway, having been invited in previously. He walked to her, placed his hand on her shoulder, and smiled. "You are beautiful just the way you are."

"But..." Seeing her friend's determined look, she assented and put her arm through Kane's.

Mia was overwhelmed by the grandeur of Brogio's estate as the carriage pulled by four black Friesians entered the huge black gates. The main house glowed as hundreds of candle lit lanterns sat in the windows, down the entryway steps and flanked the driveway. She had never seen a home that looked more like a palace.

Brogio stood just outside the doorway, and she was intrigued by his handsome face and body. The consummate host, he whisked her inside and wined and dined her. As she picked at a sweet cake on a stomach that hadn't had this much food in months, she became instantly fearful when he made his proposition of vampirism. "No! I couldn't possibly consider something this degrading!" She rose to leave, but Kane placed his hand on hers.

"You couldn't consider the possibility of having great strength, longevity and time to accumulate wealth, with my help?"

She slowly sat back down and turned to her former love interest. "Are... are... you... a... vampire, too?"

Kane smiled. "Yes, but only by my own choice. Brogio isn't a monster. He proposes to create an army to destroy those who are monsters, slashing and killing innocent humans."

They talked through the night. The appeal of being independent and having an opportunity to create wealth spoke to her in ways she hadn't thought possible.

Finally, after hours of deliberation, Mia turned to Kane. "Only if you do it, Kane. You be the one to turn me."

Kane, who had never been known for his patience, took her in his embrace before she had time to change her mind.

The following night, Kane sat on his stool at work and thought about approaching da Vinci. The master wasn't old, but the manner in which he lived his life and his extreme intelligence gave him the aura of being more aged.

He watched the master, whose mind seemed to be consumed by his fascination for everything in the universe, struggle to paint his mural. "Master, what would you do if you could live eternally?

Da Vinci hesitated in mid-stroke at the wall and turned to Kane. "Why, I imagine I would continue to invent and study just as I am now." The genius shrugged and went back to his mural.

Kane thought of the possibilities with da Vinci living as a vampire and knew that he wouldn't be able to continue with the patronage he enjoyed from the Medicis, the Borgias, and King Francis of France. This required travel during daylight to them, which would be impossible. Even if Brogio applied his great wealth to assist da Vinci, he knew in his heart that the great man wouldn't see the reasoning. He shrugged it off as a bad idea. Some part of him wanted the master inventor to remain himself entirely.

Instead, he concentrated on his black sheep cousin Marco de Medici. Tracking him down, Kane feigned an accidental meeting at a popular alehouse. "Marco, just the man I've been wanting to see." Kane slapped his cousin on the back. "How would you like to strengthen your chances at advancement?

Marco, a blonde, blue-eyed man of regular height, winked at his cousin. "I'm always up for any adventure that puts coin in my pocket and advances my ability to get ahead. What do you have in mind?"

"Come with me." Kane pointed to the doorway.

"After you." Marco smiled.

They sat together in Brogio's den next to a roaring fire. Brogio stood before the fire as Marco and Kane sat across from each other in identical overstuffed chairs.

"You have always craved power, Marco. This will bring it to you." Kane leaned forward and smiled, lowering his fangs for Marco to observe.

Marco had fewer questions than all the others. It was true, he craved power. The life of a vampire thrilled him. "I have but two questions."

"Ask away." Kane jumped up to pour the three of them more wine.

"Will I still function as a man with women, and will I have a will of my own?"

Brogio interjected. "You will be as you are only one-hundred times better. By becoming one of us, you will pledge your undying allegiance to your maker, Kane. In doing so, you are also beholden to me, Kane's sire, as your ultimate master. However," Brogio held up a finger as Marco started to interrupt, "you will have free will. By being faithful to us, you will be rewarded beyond your wildest dreams."

Marco took the wine glass that Kane offered, swallowed it in one gulp, stood, and said, "Let's do this."

Eight became sixteen. Sixteen became sixty-four. Sixty-four became five hundred.

But Calliope's rippers increased in number as well.

Every day both armies grew.

∞

Brogio and Kane's brood swore an eternal vow to uphold Brogio's rules and eradicate Italy of rippers.

In exchange, with access to Brogio's excessive wealth and contacts, they would be able to lead their own covens and build a comfortable life, existing as they could not as humans.

Brogio laid out the strategy for the initial group of eight including Kane and himself. His thought process was approached with military precision.

They stood in his den in front of the roaring fire as he gave them his simple instructions. *Rippers are mindless blood machines that live only to kill and drink human blood. The more they kill, the more they crave. We must stop them. Each night, make it a goal to convince and turn one person. In turn, each of you will continue that goal. It is imperative that you stay with them to ensure they will be able to control and satisfy their blood lust. Rule them with iron fists until you feel they can be trusted.*

Only let them prey upon the vilest of humanity, never an innocent. I will spend the next several weeks teaching you how to control your own blood lust and that of your progeny. As you confront rippers, eradicate them. Take their heads or their hearts. Use pure silver or wood. That will end them.

In less than a month, the eight of them grew to ten thousand. Like a bad cold, each human infected spread the disease to others. As they grew, they spread out through Italy, and because the rippers killed mindlessly, often murdering instead of turning their prey, they didn't grow as quickly. They soon had reduced the number of rippers to fewer than several hundred.

Shortly after the strategic plan was in place, Kane began to track down Calliope. Strangely, she hadn't gone too far afield from where they first met. He found her in Lucca, an hour from Florence. Watching her from afar, he observed her try and charm an unsuspecting young man who looked to be English rather than Italian. Just as she guided her prey into an alleyway, Kane used his speed and strength to grab her by the waist. Her intended victim sprang forward and ran off as she released him.

"You! Let me go." She gnashed her fangs at Kane's arms. One quick chop to the head rendered her unconscious. He bound and gagged her and hoisted her in an awaiting carriage. Every time she moved, he wacked her in the head throughout the hour's drive to Brogio's estate.

She fought him like a hellcat when he drug her out of the carriage and through the estate door into the den. Brogio grabbed her by the neck and held her with one arm in the air. Her legs and arms tried to strike him, but Kane had her tightly bound.

So this is the woman who began all our problems. Brogio shook his head and sighed. He then promptly dropped her on the floor, and she let out a cry. *Why in the world didn't you just compel her when you realized she had turned, Kane?*

Kane shook his head and walked over to the crystal wine bar to pour a glass of merlot. *It shocked me to see that she had turned. Rattled is probably a better word. I turned and ran from her, hoping she'd just disappear, I guess.*

Brogio stared down at Calliope. Her eyes stabbed into his, and he locked onto them. *You will stop struggling.*

The ripper's body instantly stopped moving.

Brogio placed his right foot on her stomach, reached down to her chest, and pushed his fingers into it.

Calliope's screams echoed throughout the house.

With one swift movement, he ripped her heart from her body and threw it into the roaring fire, which sputtered as it consumed the blackened organ. Looking up at Kane, he commanded, *Take her body and burn it behind the winery.*

With the flick of his wrist, Brogio had rendered the opposition army leaderless.

∞

The six coven leaders gathered together after six months of ripper annihilation at Brogio's Tuscany estate with Brogio and Kane. Brogio's servants, now all kindred, had arranged six additional chairs in horseshoe fashion facing the fire in the estate den.

"The country is rid of ripper activity, Father." Alexander took pride in the fact that he turned the greatest of the Pope's Army into members of his coven. They were skilled warriors against which the rippers stood little chance.

"I am greatly pleased, Alexander, with all of you." Brogio stood with his back straight in front of the fire and raised his right arm and pointed to each coven leader — Ian, Leslie, Joseph, Mia, Marco and finally Alexander - in return. "Now is the time for your reward."

His kindred gathered closer to the fire in the den. Leslie sat on Ian's lap in one of the large, plush chairs. Joseph nudged Kane playfully as Brogio's eldest blood son tried to pour a glass of wine. Alexander stood at attention behind one of the additional chairs. Marco eyed Mia admiringly and pointed for her to take a seat in the companion fireside chair.

Brogio eyed his soldier commander. "Alexander, you will control a most appropriate region of Italy, I think, the Centre with Rome at its heart."

Alexander saluted and smiled in spite of his stern visage.

"Ian and Leslie," Brogio smiled at them as they snuggled in the chair. "I think you will be most happy in the islands, with Palermo as your base."

Leslie giggled, and Ian hugged her and smiled at his maker.

"Joseph, you will most fit into the southern life around Naples." Brogio rubbed his chin. "You will love the lightheartedness of the people there."

Joseph nudged Kane and gave him a wink.

"Marco and Mia, you will prosper in the Northeast near Bologna. It is metropolitan and has much opportunity for you both to prosper and grow."

The two looked at each other. Marco spoke for them both. "It's not that we aren't grateful, but why do we have to divide the region? We are not a couple."

"Ah, Marco, that is where you are wrong. I have large holdings in Bologna, and I will need both of you to run them. Do you not see the attraction that runs between you?" Brogio pushed back silver strands of hair behind his ears.

Marco glanced at Mia and smiled. He offered her his hand. "Well, partner, shall we work together?"

Mia smiled and took his hand.

Brogio turned to Kane. "The northwest is yours, my son. You will thrive in Milan. It is destined to provide you with a spectacular future."

Kane drained his wine glass and stepped forward toward Brogio. "No, Father, I want to stay here in Florence with you. This is where my studies are with da Vinci. Let someone else take what you have offered."

Brogio frowned. "Milan will be a leading global city with strengths in art, commerce, design, education, entertainment, finance, fashion, and research. It will be a mecca for universities and education. Da Vinci will work there. Soon. I want you to go with him. I have seen this in my visions. You must trust me. You need to be there at the beginning of its growth."

"But... " Kane hesitated for a moment. "I told you what was important to me. What if your visions aren't reality? In Florence, I have what I need now."

"Always so impatient, my son." Brogio sighed.

"If this is my reward, I don't want it." Kane sat down his wine glass. "What I want is the ability to have true free will. If I can't stay here with you in Florence, then I want to see the world on my own, as you have."

Brogio rubbed his right hand down his face in aggravation. "Do you not believe that I know what is best for you?" Violet eyes that intermittently turned red stared into dark ones.

"I want you to give me my freedom. I will be at your beck and call should you need me. All you have to do is think me here, and I will be." Kane stood up tall and defiant. He desired to be the exception to the rule.

"And all I wanted was your companionship and loyalty. I am willing to send you to Milan for the sake of your own future. That unto itself is giving up the companionship I desired. Now you want to travel away even further?"

"For a time, Brogio." Kane walked to Brogio's side. I will end my apprenticeship with da Vinci and use my new abilities to discover and prosper. Give me your blessing."

Blood father and son locked eyes. The coven leaders left one by one to let this work out between Brogio and Kane. Soon they remained alone in the room, the only sound the fire crackling behind them.

Brogio sighed. "If this is what you want... use your gifts wisely. Stick to the rules. But promise me that you will come whenever I call you."

"I promise. I will always be at your side whenever you need me." Kane touched Brogio's arm. "Shall we sit and enjoy another glass of wine together?"

"Yes, your loyalty in the recent past is deserving of my forgiveness. But, promise me one thing." Brogio looked deeply into his kindred's eyes.

Kane returned the gaze. "Whatever you wish."

Brogio turned to the wine bar and poured them each a full glass of Boudreaux. "You will understand and obey my rules going forward."

"Yes, Father."

Kane felt wrapped in a blanket of sadness. He would miss Brogio and struggled inwardly wondering if he shouldn't leave. Yet, he sensed that he could travel and gain knowledge that would someday be useful to Brogio.

Brogio raised his glass to Kane. "To your future. To our future, and all that it holds for us."

The End

To learn how Kane's accumulated knowledge helps to save Brogio and his loved ones time and time again, discover the Snow Blood Series. Look for more adventures with Kane in the Moon Blood Series coming soon.

If you enjoyed "Kane" please consider leaving a review! Thank you!

Continue on with next book:

http://mybook.to/SB1

Keep reading for a sneak peek of Snow Blood:

Season 1!

Snow Blood is the epic story of the first vampire as told through the eyes of his kindred dog.

When Brogio must turn Snow, a beautiful white husky, in order to save the dog, a series of events are unleashed that reveal a sinister plot against the father of all vampires.

As life and true death experiences bond the master vampire and his newly transformed vampire canine together, they unravel a conspiracy that when resolved may return Selene, the love of Brogio's life, back to him and set him free from the lonely existence that has plagued him for thousands of years.

Episode One : Transformation

The pain sliced into my ribs like steel on bone. Then, nothingness.

Searing pain, and the sight of two snarling, rabid beasts locked in battle, interrupted the safety of my void. The scent of their blood-filled rage made my nose twitch. My brain screamed "move" but my legs disobeyed. Paralyzed on the ground, I watched as two giant beasts circled each other, lumbering dangerously close. One, an unknown, unnatural brother who could stand on hind legs. The other ... a demon, perhaps? That was the best way I could describe this otherworldly creature.

My eyes began to focus. I could see blood-covered fangs and claws, a demon strangely glowing in the lunar light. It looked "moon-kissed". Light from the night-time sun caressed this deformed creature. Perhaps I'm imagining this? Maybe it's my love of the moon. I've always felt its protection at night on my forays into the woods near my home.

Jaws snapping. The upright wolf-being lunged. The demon creature moved faster, almost a blur. It hastily side-stepped the wolf's bite as easily as a mongoose avoids a cobra. The wolf snarled its frustration. It circled the moon-kissed demon that appeared to be taunting its opponent. I tried to move to observe better, but pain savagely raked through me. A dark circle of wetness surrounded me. The air reeked with the smell of ... blood. My blood.

Why had I recklessly left the comfort of my home? The fireplace in the den warmed us against the outside of fall's cold weather. Perhaps I needed adventure. Prey lurked in the outside darkness, and instinctively, I had wanted to give chase. My little human tried to tackle me just as I dashed to the kitchen and nosed aside the flap from the back door to the freedom of the night that beckoned me.

"Snow! Don't go out there. It's dark!" He squirmed, trying to hold me. He weighed less than any little subaltern laying his body across my shaggy mass. Embarrassing, I thought, since I outranked him in the pack. But, I never snapped at him. My little human needed my protection.

"Let him go, Tommy. He's just doing his job; keeping the coyotes away." Tommy's father, our Alpha, had spoken, and we must all obey.

The little human stood upright and slowly released his grip on my back. Moments later, I was chasing coyotes across the front lawn and out into the street, doing what I did best – protecting my pack. Now, as the sound of gnashing teeth brought me back into the present, I wished for the chance to better safeguard them. Who would warn my humans of this danger if I didn't make it home?

The two creatures battled on. The wolf leaped over its combatant's head, narrowly avoiding a crushing blow to its leg. The glowing demon blurred, quickly avoiding an attack from the rear. It spun just in time to avoid its throat from being taken. Suddenly, fall leaves were flying into the air.

They hit the grass under the trees that lined the abandoned road and tumbled, arms and heads over legs.

My paws quivered as the fight drew closer to me. Inexplicitly, I remained unable to move from where I had landed after the pain hit me. My energy had already seeped from my body. Running away appeared no longer an option.

I watched as the fierce beasts arose quickly from their tumble. The wolf gained an advantage, lunging forward and extending its claws as the demon stumbled over a broken tree trunk. Its opportune fall to the ground enabled the demon to duck the razor-sharp claws. Just missing the demon, the wolf landed and rolled behind its enemy. Quickly, it spun up to go after its prey now sprawled out on the grass.

Just as the wolf leaped, BOOM. A loud explosion ... and then the wolf crumpled to the ground with a pained yelp and a heavy thud. His lifeless body sprawled awkwardly on the dirt.

A strange voice pierced through my head. "Silver bullets work well on panweres, too." A malicious chuckle followed.

Was that the demon's voice? I wondered. Surely I did not see his lips moving.

The demon creature knelt over its victim and poked the wolf's body. No sign of life. Triumphantly, it threw back its head and let out a victory scream that made the hairs on my neck bristle. It then rose to cast its appraising gaze in my direction. I struggled to get my feet under me, fearing that if I didn't, the demon would kill me on this spot, just as he had taken the life of the wolf. As it approached me, I felt my life slowly drain away; the darkness enveloped me again. The sadness of never seeing my family again lingered ...

Darkness closed over me ... drifting into ... an overwhelming itchy sensation? My nerve endings were on fire, consuming me with a new-found rush. The thin line of life spread throughout me. Every fiber of my body stood on end as the blood-filled eyes of the demon pierced mine. A thin drop of blood clung to one of its fangs before descending onto my face in slow motion. I tried to move but the creature held me in place with one giant claw-covered hand. Other than the weight of its massive body, I felt no trace of the initial pain that had sent me into darkness.

I watched transfixed as the creature transformed into a human. First claws became large hands. It shrunk only slightly. Its deformed body took the shape of a strong, muscular athlete. Its distorted visage faded into a handsome face with a strong nose, cheek bones and jaw. It was only seconds until it became a naked man. It spoke.

"Hold still, dog. Let your body absorb my venom and heal."

Venom? Heal me? Fire streaked through my veins, forcing every part of me to come alive. An unfamiliar strength enveloped me. I had been crippled only moments ago. Now, every part of me sprang to life. My eyes never left the demon/man.

Blonde and fair, a pale face framed large violet-colored eyes that transitioned back to red and again to violet. He towered over me; his long, muscular frame stretched over what must have been almost a half-head taller than James, my master. I once heard my master brag, "I'm six-foot-one in my stocking feet." I guess that was his way of stating how tall he is.

The demon/man wiped the blood from his face onto his hand. My blood, or his? I wasn't sure.

"All right," he commanded, "try to get up now."

I sprang to all fours, shook my heavy white coat and sat back on my haunches. How did I get on this deserted road in the middle of the woods? Prey. That's it. Chasing prey. The large black car with Oregon plates sitting sideways in the road next to us, lights on, motor running, looked as though it had swerved to avoid something. Had it collided with me?

The man knelt down and patted my head. "Confused are you? That's right, I hit you."

I cocked my head at him, feeling better than before. How could he have hit me? I got a whiff of his odor. A layer of perfume concealed the smell of death and something rotten that had emanated from the demon during its battle with the wolf. I stood and shook my whole body again, as if to expel the experience and the smell. Then I turned away to go back home.

"Wait!" He placed a firm grip on my back with his strong, human hands.

I whipped my head around, baring teeth in warning. Let me go! I had to go home to my loving family and the warm fire that awaited me.

He stared at me. "No, that's an insane thought."

Was he speaking to me? Was he reading my mind?

He paused for a long moment, staring at me as if he could see through me. I shivered from the menacing touch of his hand on my back.

He released his grip. His shoulders slumped, and he ran a bloody hand through his blonde hair. He took a long, deep breath, then shook his head. "Come with me."

I watched him move toward the car. I had to go home. My people must be worried.

He turned to me, and I felt drawn to him. No, I must go home.

"There is no choice, dog. Come with me."

No! The hackles on my back stood on end in warning. I will go home! I backed away, growling in defiance. I turned to run, but he blocked my path to freedom and caught me in a heartbeat.

He stopped me in my tracks. How could this human outrun me?

He grabbed my head with his bloody hands and twisted my face to meet his blood-red eyes. "You will come with me now! It is for your survival and that of your people." He let go and stood tall again. He took two long strides to the car. Over his shoulder he commanded, "Come!"

I resisted with everything that I had.

He opened a door to the large sedan and motioned for me to take the passenger seat. I tried to resist again but my legs disobeyed me, and I covered the short space and jumped in. He slammed the door behind me.

I growled as I watched him cross in front of the car and open the driver's door. A black turtleneck sweater and black pants hung on the back of the driver's seat. Black loafers and socks sat on the floor in front of the seat. He reached inside for them and hurriedly put them on, never taking his eyes from me. His gaze was creeping me out. Intense.

Sliding behind the wheel, he looked at me for a long minute. "You're my responsibility now. Let's go find you something to eat. You will need your strength."

I didn't like his toothy grin. What wasn't he telling me?

I found it odd that my ravenous cravings for something ... something very bloody outweighed all other reason.

∞

Continue reading Snow Blood: Season 1! Purchase
your copy here: http://mybook.to/SB1

Thank you for reading *Kane*. Reviews are a tremendous help for authors. If you enjoyed this book, writing a review would be a huge boon.

Want more stories from the eyes of a dog? Join the exclusive readers group for GIVEAWAYS, Advanced reader opportunities and Pre-order notifications!

Join here: http://eepurl.com/bAuq2b

Connect with Carol McKibben:

Facebook:

https://www.facebook.com/CarolMckibbenAuthor

Twitter:

https://twitter.com/CarolMcKibben

AUTHOR WEBSITE:

http://www.carolmckibben.com/

About the Author:

Carol McKibben was a magazine publisher for 20+ years. Carol writes from the heart of a dog's eyes. Her books help support her dog rescue efforts and focus on unconditional love.

Carol, her labradoodle Neo, lab Thor and Siberian Husky Ty are currently working on new adventures.

Go to http://www.carolmckibben.com or email carol@mckibben.com.